Illustration by YUEWEI SHI

To the heroes who walked before me,
and inspired all of us to dream big!
K.Y.

First published in the United States of America by Dial Books for Young Readers,
an imprint of Penguin Random House LLC, 2022

Text copyright © 2022 by Yang Yang

Title page and endpaper illustrations
© 2022 Yuewei Shi
Pages 3-4 illustration © 2022 Sally Deng
Pages 5-6 illustration © 2022 Dow Phumiruk
Pages 7-8 illustration © 2022 Dan Santat
Pages 9-10 illustration © 2022 Fahmida Azim
Pages 11-12 illustration © 2022 Yao Xiao
Pages 13-14 illustration © 2022 Julie Kwon

Pages 15-16 illustration © 2022 Nabi Ali
Pages 17-18 illustration © 2022 Yuko Shimizu
Pages 19-20 illustration © 2020 Sujean Rim
Pages 21-22 illustration © 2020 Kitkat Pecson
Pages 23-24 illustration © 2020 Nhung Lê
Pages 25-26 illustration © 2020 Shreya Gupta
Pages 27-28 illustration © 2020 Julia Kuo
Pages 29-30 illustration © 2020 Marcos Chin

Dial & colophon are registered trademarks of Penguin Random House LLC.
Visit us online at penguinrandomhouse.com.

Library of Congress Cataloging-in-Publication Data is available.

Printed in the USA • ISBN 9780593463055

1 3 5 7 9 10 8 6 4 2

PC • Design by Mina Chung
Text set in Stempel Garamond and Futura Medium and Bold

The publisher does not have any control over and does not assume
any responsibility for author or third-party websites or their content.

YES
WE
WILL

ASIAN AMERICANS WHO SHAPED THIS COUNTRY

KELLY YANG

ILLUSTRATED BY

NABI H. ALI • FAHMIDA AZIM • MARCOS CHIN • SALLY DENG • SHREYA GUPTA

JULIA KUO • JULIE KWON • NHUNG LÊ • KITKAT PECSON • DOW PHUMIRUK

SUJEAN RIM • DAN SANTAT • YUKO SHIMIZU • YAO XIAO • YUEWEI SHI

DIAL BOOKS FOR YOUNG READERS

Illustration by SALLY DENG

A long time ago, our ancestors came to this land to build a better life. To build a better future.

20,000 Chinese American immigrants building the
TRANSCONTINENTAL RAILROAD amid dangerous conditions

They were told to get out.
They were told they couldn't stay.

Illustration by DOW PHUMIRUK

You know what they said to that?
They said, we belong here and we will thrive!
"Yes, we will!"

Early Asian American immigrants faced many discriminatory
laws and orders, including the **CHINESE EXCLUSION ACT**,
the Foreigner's Miners Tax, the Page Act of 1875, and others.

We'll soar to high heights.

JEREMY LIN, National
Basketball Association player

PHILIP VERA CRUZ, labor
leader and civil rights activist

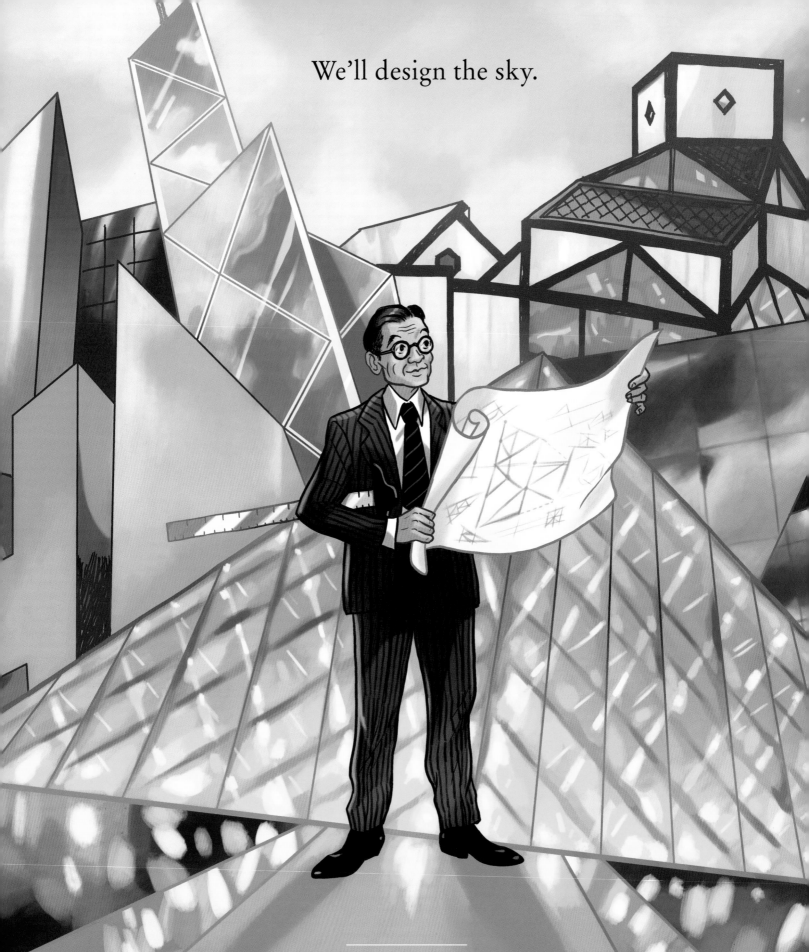

We'll design the sky.

I. M. PEI, architect

Illustration by YAO XIAO

And jet off to space!

FRANKLIN CHANG-DÍAZ, NASA astronaut

We'll defend our country.

Serve the people.

TAMMY DUCKWORTH, United States senator
and former Army National Guard lieutenant colonel

KAMALA HARRIS,
Vice president of the United States
and former United States senator

And protect our loved ones.

Illustration by JULIE KWON

PETER TSAI, scientist
and inventor of the
N95 mask

We'll strive for equality!

MAMIE TAPE, eight-year-old Chinese American girl who fought against school segregation

FRED TOYOSABURO KOREMATSU,
activist who resisted the Japanese internment
order during World War II

Illustration by YUKO SHIMIZU

And look good while doing it.

VERA WANG,
fashion designer

Illustration by SUJEAN RIM

We'll dance from our souls!

LIA CIRIO, ballet dancer
and choreographer

We'll write breathtaking, amazing stories.

JENNY HAN,
author

Illustrations by
KITKAT PECSON

Speak truth to power.

AMANDA NGUYEN,
social entrepreneur, activist

STAND UP
SPEAK UP

RISE

RISE UP

Bring audiences
  laughter, tears . . .

SANDRA OH, actor

and all-around hope.

SUNISA LEE,
gymnast and
Olympian

Illustrations by NHUNG LÊ

Daydream through our fingers,

YO-YO MA,
cellist

Illustrations by SHREYA GUPTA

and sing our hearts out.

H.E.R.,
singer and
songwriter

And oh how we will cook!

PADMA LAKSHMI,
author, activist, and chef

Illustration by
JULIA KUO

Glorious meals that bring us together,
to celebrate all the things that make us unique.

For we can be
ANYTHING.

Illustration by MARCOS CHIN

All we have to do is dream it.

AUTHOR'S NOTE

From 1863 to 1869, roughly 20,000 Chinese laborers helped build the 1,776-mile **TRANSCONTINENTAL RAILROAD**, connecting the Pacific coast with the Atlantic. The workers labored through boiling summers and freezing winters, drilling tunnels thirty feet deep in the snowy mountains and shoveling pounds of rock to make their way through the Sierra Nevada mountains. Hundreds died from the treacherous conditions. Despite putting their lives on the line day in and day out, they were paid 30 to 50 percent lower wages than white workers and made to pay for their own food. In 1895, Leland Stanford, president of Central Pacific Railroad company, former California governor and founder of Stanford University, told Congress, "The majority of the railroad labor force were Chinese. Without them, it would be impossible to complete the western portion of this great national enterprise, within the time required by the Acts of Congress."

Early Asian American immigrants faced many discriminatory laws, including the **CHINESE EXCLUSION ACT**, which banned Chinese laborers, both skilled and unskilled, from entering the country. It made Chinese immigrants ineligible for citizenship and naturalization, giving them the legal status of permanent "aliens." The Act was passed in response to years of anti-immigrant hostility and violence on the part of Americans who feared the new immigrants would take their jobs. Seven years earlier, Congress had passed the Page Act of 1875, which banned Chinese women from emigrating to the United States, but the Chinese Exclusion Act went even further, taking away rights from existing immigrants. If Chinese immigrants were not allowed to be citizens, they could not challenge discriminatory laws like this. The repercussions were immediate, as xenophobic Americans launched the "Driving Out" period, physically forcing Chinese people out of their towns. The Rock Springs massacre of 1885 and the Hells Canyon massacre of 1887 are both chilling reminders of the social and physical impact of the Act.

JEREMY LIN (b. 1988) is a Taiwanese American professional basketball player. Born and raised in California, he is the first American of Chinese or Taiwanese descent to play in the National Basketball Association, and the first Asian American to win an NBA Championship. While playing for the New York Knicks, Lin led the team to seven straight wins and ten wins in thirteen games, causing the cultural phenomenon "Linsanity" to sweep the nation. Lin averaged 22.3 points and 9 assists per game during this winning streak. To the next generation of Asian American ballers, Lin says, "When you get your shot, do NOT hesitate. Don't worry whether anyone else thinks you belong. When you get your foot in the door, KICK THAT DOOR DOWN. And then bring others up with you."

PHILIP VERA CRUZ (1904–1994) was a Filipino American labor leader, farmworker, and civil rights activist. Cruz worked as a farmworker in Delano, California, in the 1940s, picking grapes, lettuce, and asparagus in the blistering 110-degree heat for nine to ten hours a day with no access to healthcare, benefits, or other rights on the job. In 1965, Cruz led the Delano Grape Strike to demand a ten cents an hour increase in pay. The strike caught national and international attention, becoming one of the most important movements in the history of farmworkers' rights, and leading to the birth of United Farm Workers Union (UFW). According to Cruz, "If more young people could just get involved in the important issues of social justice, they would form a golden foundation for the struggle of all people to improve their lives."

I. M. PEI (1917–2019) was a Chinese American architect. A "bold yet pragmatic" architect born in China and educated in the United States, he designed some of the most iconic buildings in the world, including the Louvre Pyramid in Paris, France; the Bank of China Tower in Hong Kong; the Museum of Islamic Art in Doha, Qatar; and the John F. Kennedy Presidential Library and Museum in Boston, Massachusetts, United States. Pei often had to ignore the naysayers, who doubted a Chinese American designer could and should sculpt such important buildings. "I couldn't walk the streets of Paris without people looking at me and saying, 'There you go again. What are you doing here? What are you doing to us? What are you doing to our great Louvre?'" he once said. However, he didn't let that get him down. In 1983, Pei won the Pritzker Prize, considered the highest honor a living architect can receive. He used the $100,000 award to establish a scholarship fund for Chinese architecture students.

FRANKLIN CHANG-DÍAZ (b. 1950) is a Costa Rican Chinese American astronaut. As a young boy in Costa Rica, Chang-Díaz always knew he wanted to be an astronaut. After immigrating to the US, Díaz received a full-ride scholarship to the University of Connecticut; however, the university soon said they made a mistake. "They told me, 'You deserve this scholarship, but you are not a US citizen. We thought that you were from Puerto Rico, not Costa Rica,'" said Chang-Díaz. His high school teachers petitioned the Connecticut legislature, and he was allowed to go to university on a one-year scholarship. To pay for the rest, Chang-Díaz worked in the university's physics department. His background in physics proved useful later in life. A veteran of seven space shuttle missions, he is tied with astronaut Jerry L. Ross for the record of the most spaceflights. To future astronauts, Díaz's advice is to "find one's own dream and to most importantly, follow it. The only way for the dream to come true is to really want it and chase after it."

TAMMY DUCKWORTH (b. 1968) is a Thai American United States senator and former Army National Guard lieutenant colonel. The daughter of a Vietnam War veteran, Duckworth started working at the age of sixteen to support her family. While at George Washington University, she enlisted in the army, training as a helicopter pilot. In 2004, she was sent to Iraq, where her helicopter was shot down by a grenade. Duckworth lost both her legs and some mobility in her right arm. She was awarded the Purple Heart. Elected to the House of Representatives in 2013, and to the United States Senate in 2016, Duckworth holds many "firsts." She's the first Thai American woman and the first woman with a disability elected to Congress. She's also the first female double amputee in the Senate and the first senator to give birth while in office. She says of her wheelchair, "People always want me to hide it in pictures. I say no! I earned this wheelchair. It's no different from a medal I wear on my chest. Why would I hide it?"

KAMALA HARRIS (b. 1964) is the first Asian American Black vice president of the United States. She was born in Oakland, California, to parents who emigrated from India and Jamaica. Harris became a prosecutor for the Alameda County District Attorney's Office in 2004, and then the attorney general of California in 2011. She then served as a United States senator from California from 2017 to 2021. As a senator, she advocated for healthcare reform and immigrants' rights, among other issues. During the 2020 election, Harris ran for United States president, and soon accepted President Joe Biden's invitation to become his running mate. Though she is the first woman, the first Black American, and the first Asian American to be elected vice president, she is determined not to be the last. "To the children of our country," says Harris. "Dream with ambition, lead with conviction, and see yourself in a way that others might not see you, simply because they've never seen it before. And we will applaud you every step of the way."

PETER TSAI (b. 1952) is a Taiwanese American scientist who invented the N95 mask filter. During the COVID-19 pandemic, the N95 mask, which can block 95 percent of particles, has been instrumental in helping doctors and nurses combat the pandemic and protect billions of lives. Tsai grew up on a family farm in Taichung, Taiwan, before immigrating to the United States in 1981. A prolific inventor, he holds more than twelve US patents and over twenty commercial license agreements. In 1992, while at the University of Tennessee, Tsai led a research team to develop the N95 filter. When the COVID-19 pandemic hit, he came out of retirement to test new ways to sterilize the masks. According to his daughters, Tsai says, "it's not only about the quality of the work you do, but how you make a difference for the people you work with and the final result of your accomplishments."

MAMIE TAPE (1876–1934), a Chinese American activist, was eight years old when she fought against school segregation in San Francisco, California, in 1885, numerous decades before the *Mendez vs. Westminster* and *Brown vs. Board of Education* cases. Born to Chinese immigrants, Mamie Tape tried to enroll in the all-white Spring Valley Primary School in 1884, but Principal Jennie Hurley refused to admit her, citing school board policy prohibiting Chinese children from attending the city's public schools. Mamie's parents decided to sue the San Francisco Board of Education. In a letter to the *Alta California* newspaper, Mary Tape, Mamie's mother, wrote, "Dear sirs. Will you please tell me! Is it a disgrace to be born a Chinese? Didn't God make us all!!!" The lawsuit went all the way to the California Supreme Court, which eventually ruled in favor of the Tapes and required public education to be open to all children. Though Mamie subsequently attended the newly established Chinese Primary School, her siblings got to attend public school in Berkeley, California. Her case and ruling were instrumental to opening the door for more and more Chinese children to attend formerly all-white schools.

FRED TOYOSABURO KOREMATSU (1919–2005) was a Japanese American activist who resisted the Japanese internment order during World War II. On February 19, 1942, President Franklin D. Roosevelt issued Executive Order 9066 following the attack on Pearl Harbor, and ordered the detention of 120,000 people of Japanese ancestry, even those who were US citizens. Though the rest of his family obeyed the order, Korematsu refused. He adopted a fake identity and even underwent plastic surgery to try to change his appearance. However, the police soon arrested him on suspicion that he was Japanese. At his trial in federal court in San Francisco, Korematsu challenged the constitutionality of the order. He appealed his case all the way to the United States Supreme Court, and though Korematsu ultimately lost, his heroic effort shined a light on the devastating effects of legalizing racism. He successfully lobbied Congress to pass the Civil Liberties Act of 1988. In 1998, he was awarded the Presidential Medal of Freedom. According to Korematsu: "If you have the feeling that something is wrong, don't be afraid to speak up."

VERA WANG (b. 1949) is a Chinese American fashion designer. Born and raised in New York City to Chinese immigrants, Wang initially wanted to become a competitive ice skater. When she didn't make the 1968 US Olympic team, she turned to fashion instead. Wang became one of the youngest editors of *Vogue* magazine, where she worked for seventeen years. With an editor's eye, she went on to transform the bridal market, designing wedding gowns for Chelsea Clinton, Alicia Keys, Jennifer Lopez, and many others. Her training as a figure skater helped inspire her collections, and she was inducted into the US Figure Skating Hall of Fame in 2009 for her contribution as a costume designer to the sport. Wang's designs now include ready-to-wear clothing and evening wear, which frequently appear on the red carpet at the Academy Awards. Her career advice for the next generation is: "Do something you really love. It doesn't matter what it is. If you love it, it'll get you through the hard times."

LIA CIRIO (b. 1986) is a Filipina American dancer and choreographer. She started dancing when she was three years old. At the age of sixteen, she was invited to join Boston Ballet II, and in 2010 became a principal ballerina. At Boston Ballet II, she performed over one hundred lead roles, including featured and/or principal roles in classics such as *Cinderella, Swan Lake, Giselle, Sleeping Beauty,* and many more. In 2018, she made her debut as a choreographer and started the Cirio Collective to encourage new choreography. Though Cirio encountered biases in ballet as an Asian American, she remains hopeful. "Audiences now, they are not coming to see a pure white ballerina, they can imagine an Asian person being a swan or a Black person being a Giselle," says Cirio.

JENNY HAN (b. 1980) is a Korean American author. She's the #1 *New York Times* bestselling author of the To All the Boys series. All three books were adapted into Netflix movies, on which she served as an executive producer. *To All the Boys I've Loved Before* is one of Netflix's most viewed original movies ever. Han is also the author of the Summer I Turned Pretty series (to be adapted into a television series for Amazon), among other books. Her stories have been published in more than thirty languages. A former librarian, Han speaks widely on the importance of representation. "What would it have meant for me back then to see a girl who looked like me star in a movie? Not as the sidekick or romantic interest, but as the lead? Not just once, but again and again? Everything," wrote Han in the *New York Times*.

AMANDA NGUYEN (b. 1991) is a Vietnamese American social entrepreneur, civil rights activist, astronaut in training, and the founder and CEO of Rise, a non-governmental civil rights organization. The daughter of Vietnamese boat refugees, Nguyen credits her immigrant upbringing with shaping her courage in the fight for justice. As a survivor, she wrote the Sexual Assault Survivors' Bill of Rights, safeguarding the right for survivors to have a rape kit at no cost and the requirement that kits be preserved for twenty years. The bill unanimously passed into federal law in 2016. Her organization, Rise, advocates for survivors and assists people to write and pass their own bills. When anti-Asian hate skyrocketed during the COVID-19 pandemic, Nguyen took to social media, making viral videos that kickstarted the movement to stop violence against Asian Americans. For all her activism, Nguyen was nominated for a Nobel Peace Prize in 2019. According to Nguyen: "The greatest tool we all have is our voice."

SANDRA OH (b. 1971) is a Korean Canadian American actress. Born in Ontario, Canada, to Korean immigrant parents, Oh wanted to pursue an acting career from a young age. Despite her parents' initial disapproval, she persevered, and has gone on to star in supporting or lead roles in more than fifty films and thirty television shows, including *Grey's Anatomy*, *Killing Eve*, and *The Chair*. In 2019, she became the first actress of Asian descent to be nominated for the Primetime Emmy Award for Outstanding Lead Actress in a Drama Series, the first Asian woman to host the Golden Globes, and the first Asian woman to win two Golden Globes. While at the Emmy Awards, Oh famously said: "It's an honor just to be Asian." She also gave an emotional speech at the Stop Asian Hate rally in Pennsylvania in 2021, in response to the Atlanta spa shootings, leading the crowd to chant, "I am proud to be Asian! I belong here!"

SUNISA "SUNI" LEE (b. 2003) is a Hmong American gymnast and winner of the Olympic gold medal for the women's all-around in the 2020 Tokyo Olympics. The first Hmong American to compete in the Olympics, Lee began her gymnastics career with a mattress and a piece of wood which her father used to build her a "balance beam" in their yard. Young Suni went on to join the junior national team. Just two days before the 2019 National Championships, her father fell from a ladder while helping a neighbor trim a tree, and became paralyzed from the chest down. The shocking accident, along with the toll of multiple injuries to Suni's leg and foot, dealing with Internet trolls, and coping with tragedy—she lost an aunt and uncle to COVID-19—made Suni incredibly stressed before her big event at the Tokyo Olympics. But she told herself to get out there and do "nothing more, nothing less . . . because my normal is good enough. I just need to do what I usually do." And she was right.

YO-YO MA (b. 1955) is a Chinese American cellist. Born in Paris and educated in New York City, he has recorded more than ninety albums, for which he has been awarded eighteen Grammy Awards. In addition to playing classical music, Ma has recorded American bluegrass music, traditional Chinese melodies, and Brazilian music. He has played in the soundtracks of many movies, including *Crouching Tiger, Hidden Dragon*. A United Nations Messenger of Peace, Ma started his own collective in 1998 called the Silk Road Ensemble, which brings together musicians from the lands historically connected by the Silk Road in Asia. As Ma states at the beginning of his music video cover of "Prelude" from *Bach's Cello Suite No. 1*, "Culture—the way we express ourselves and understand each other—can bind us together as one world."

H.E.R., born Gabriella Sarmiento Wilson (b. 1997), is a Black Filipina American singer and songwriter. Born in California to a Filipina mother and African American father, H.E.R. started singing and performing when she was young, covering for Alicia Keys on *The Today Show* at ten years old. She has since released multiple compilations and albums that have won Grammy Awards, including for Best R&B Performance, Best R&B Album, and Song of the year and in 2021 she won the Academy Award for Best Original Song. "I'm paving the way for Black or Filipino—or both—artists to do R&B and know they don't have to compromise themselves," says the singer-songwriter.

PADMA LAKSHMI (b. 1970) is an Indian American author, cook, activist, and television host. She's the host of *Taste the Nation* and *Top Chef*, for which she received a Primetime Emmy nomination for Outstanding Reality Host in 2009. She is also the American Civil Liberties Union ambassador for immigration and women's rights. and the author of multiple cookbooks, a memoir and a children's picture book. Born in India, Lakshmi immigrated to the United States at the age of four and grew up in New York City and Los Angeles, where she struggled with "brown girl's self-loathing," caused by classmates' racist taunts and bullying. Her show *Taste the Nation* highlights and celebrates the food of American immigrants and Indigenous peoples, which often gets culturally appropriated. "I'm not just interested in the food," says Lakshmi. "I'm interested in the hand that makes the food."